The Berenstain Bears'
BIG HALLOWEEN PARTY

Skeletons, goblins, ghouls, and ghosts! Come to our party— we'll be your hosts!

The Berenstain Bears' Big Halloween Party

www.harpercollinschildrens.com
ISBN 978-0-06-302437-3
Typography by Chrisila Maida ❖
21 22 23 24 25   IMG   10 9 8 7 6 5 4 3 2 1   ❖   First Edition

BIG HALLOWEEN PARTY

Mike Berenstain

Based on the characters created by
Stan and Jan Berenstain

HARPER
An Imprint of HarperCollinsPublishers

It was autumn in Bear Country and Halloween was on its way. This year, the whole neighborhood was getting together for a big Halloween party at the Bear family's tree house. There would be a costume parade, games and refreshments, a costume contest, and trick-or-treating for all. Brother, Sister, and Honey could hardly wait!

The cubs were thinking about their costumes.
"I'm going to be a fire-breathing dragon!" said Brother.
"I'm going to be a swan-mutant superhero!" said Sister.

"I'm gonna be a big bug!" said Honey proudly.
"A bug?" asked Sister, surprised.
"Yes!" said Honey. "A ladybug!"
"Oh!" said Brother. "That will be cute."

Mama and Papa overheard the cubs.

"Excuse me," said Mama. "Where are these costumes coming from?"

"The Halloween store!" said Brother.

"I'm not sure the Halloween store has those costumes," said Papa.

"Perhaps you and Mama could help us make them!"
said Sister.

Mama and Papa looked at each other and sighed.

On Halloween day, the cubs' costumes
were ready. They were magnificent! The whole
family had, indeed, worked on them together.

The neighbors were decorating the tree house and setting out games and refreshments. The neighborhood cubs were wildly excited.

"Hmm!" said Papa. "Now we're going to fill them up with sugar and candy."

The party began with a grand costume parade. The cubs were given all sorts of noisemakers—toy horns, cow bells, pot lids to bang on, or drums to whack. They set off on a tour of the neighborhood.

TOOT! BONG! CLANG! WHOMP!
went the noisemakers.
    The cubs looked very nice in their
costumes, and they had a wonderful
time making all that noise!

When the parade got back to the tree house, everyone was
hungry and thirsty. The parents doled out refreshments and,
when everyone was refreshed, the games began.

There was bobbing for apples. Little Billy Grizzwold lost
a tooth biting into an apple.
   "Thath all right," he grinned. "It wath looth, anyway!"

Papa supervised the beanbag toss.
"Hey!" he said as a cub accidentally bounced
a beanbag off his head.
"Sorry!" said the cub.

Mama was in charge of face-painting. She did a
wonderful job. By the time she was done, the cubs'
own parents didn't recognize them!

Mr. and Mrs. Bruin ran the pin-the-bone-on-the-skeleton game and the musical tombstones game. At the end, Lizzy Bruin and Cousin Fred both sat down on the last tombstone at exactly the same moment, so it was declared a tie. The other cubs happily ran circles around Lizzy and Fred!

Next came the pumpkin piñata.
Papa held it out on a long pole for
the cubs to whack with a baseball
bat while blindfolded.

The first cub got a bit confused
and whacked Papa.

"OW!" yelled Papa.

Eventually, someone took good aim and burst the pumpkin wide open. The cubs gathered up the scattered candy while poor Papa rubbed his leg.

The party finished with a costume-judging contest. The cubs got up one at a time to display their costumes while everyone applauded. Then prizes were awarded. There were lots of prizes.

"And for the witch with the straightest hat . . ."
said Mama, giving out a prize.

"And for the dinosaur with the sharpest horn . . ."
said Papa, giving out another prize.

Soon, all the cubs had prizes and trick-or-treating
could begin.

It was getting dark and the neighborhood was looking quite spooky. There were flickering lanterns along the street. Pumpkins glowed on every porch. There were fake skeletons, ghosts, ghouls, spiders, and monsters everywhere!

The cubs set off. Parents went along with the little ones. They marched up to each front door and knocked. Some doors were old and creaky, and some houses had sound effects of shrieks and moans. It was pretty scary! But when the doors were opened, friendly neighbors were inside.

"Trick or treat!" the cubs cried and held out bags and baskets for their treats.

When the last candy bar had been gathered and the final lollipop selected, the cubs returned to the tree house to count their loot. They arranged it in neat little piles.

"Fifteen Bear Nut bars," said Brother.

"Seventeen Grizzly Pops," said Sister.

"Lots of Honey Drops!" said Honey, who couldn't count very well yet.

It was getting late. The moon was rising as the families headed home. The littlest ones were fast asleep in their parents' arms.

"Good night!" called Mama, Papa, Brother, Sister, and Honey. "Happy Halloween!"

And "Happy Halloween!" the neighbors called back.

A wonderful Halloween party had been had by all!